Montana Magic

Magic Series, Volume 1

Louise Riveiro-Mitchell

Published by Outlaws Publishing LLC, 2024.

This is a work of fiction. Similarities to real people, places, or events are entirely coincidental.

MONTANA MAGIC

First edition. June 14, 2024.

ISBN: 979-8227681836

Written by Louise Riveiro-Mitchell.

To two gentlemen that have always been an inspiration to my characters Steven Mitchell and John Wilson

Chapter 1

The mornings were getting cooler as they were preparing us for the coming of the snow still north in the high country. It was this time of year the ranchers knew their main job was to take as many hands they could spare and head to the high pastures to get the herds down before the snow blocked the pass.

From the looks of that morning sky, Jason knew they would be cutting it close. He turned and walked back into the bunk-house and poured himself a cup of coffee as the hands started to get up. As he got off his top bunk, Chet looked over to Jason, "well Boss Man, what does it look like?"

Jason turned to his best hand and smiled, "well, I tell ya if I was a betting man, I would have been headin' up to that north pass a few days ago. Ya'll see those clouds over yonder, well that means snow and it's heading this way."

UP IN THE MAIN HOUSE, Judge Elias Crawford was also looking out the window at the morning sky. Understanding the signs, he knew they had to get on the trail as soon as possible. His thoughts were interrupted by the gentle knock on the door on his study and his wife, Elizabeth, walks in with his morning coffee. "I thought a cup of nice hot coffee would help you decide if you'll be leaving for the pass today."

The judge looked at his wife, he had been married to Elizabeth Elaine Monet for almost thirty years and she was still as lovely as the first day he saw her that first day in her father's mercantile. She still was that lovely young girl, no matter how many years had passed. She smiled at him as she placed the coffee cup on his desk. He knew she would not be happy with his decision to go on the drive. Too many years have gone by, too many years, not to mention he wasn't getting any younger, but he'd like to get a few more drives under his belt. He took his wife's and sat her down on the sofa across from his desk.

"Elizabeth Dear, I've come to the decision I want to leave with the hands today to head for the north range." He saw the expression on her face and continued, "now I know what you're gonna say, but I've made up my mind Elizabeth."

Oh, Elizabeth knew he was right on that, Eli had a stubborn streak in him when he made a decision. She slowly got up and walked toward the desk and stopped, "I suppose you'll be taking all the hands."

Eli got up and placed his hands on her shoulders, he knew what she was worried about. Though they had lived here on the Circle C for the past 20 years being so far away from town, Elizabeth always had an uneasiness when everyone was gone on those yearly drives. Montana was not Kansas and they were a bit far from the civilization she grew up in. One would think after all these years, she would have changed her views, but as the saying goes, one can't take the city gal and put her in the country.

She slowly walked over to the window and without turning around, "will you be taking all the hands on this trip?"

He knew she was still a bit skittish about being left on the ranch with only a few hands. Sure there wasn't really anything to worry about and she wasn't being left with no one there besides Waco. Charlie and Bill, he's leaving Jim to help with the chores still needing to get done.

"You know we go through this each year, I thought we settled all this last year, now I can have the Johnson boys come here every afternoon just to check in on you."

She looked at him realizing how silly she was being, after all, Elias had been doing this round-up for the past sixteen years, you would think she'd be used to it by now. She gave him a smile and he kissed her forehead and together they headed for the kitchen.

As he sat down at the table, he looked at his wife and remembers when they first came to Montana. They were just a few years married when Eli decided to give up his law practice in Kansas and move out west. He had been thinking of it for some time and he had to admit the idea of starting fresh had an appeal he really was looking for. He could still practice and in a territory like Montana, he could establish himself, not only as a judge, but maybe try his hand at ranching.

And so after he convinced his wife the move was genuinely a step forward, they packed their belongings and headed west. They arrived at Fort Benton in late May and began the search for the perfect piece of land to build their future. That was eighteen years ago and the judge had built himself, not only a fine reputation for himself as a lawyer, but also had one of the finest cattle ranches in the territory. With the talk that the territory was seeking to apply for statehood, it seemed that Eli would be asked to help with the procedures to present to Washington. But for now, his attention was focused on his Elizabeth and her uneasiness on his going was a bit unnerving.

"I'll tell you what Liz, I'll ask Captain Peterson if he could spare one or two of his men until I return."

She looked at him, "you'll do no such thing Eli Crawford, we'll be fine here besides you know the captain is short-handed enough with miners up in the mountains, he needs his men right there at the fort."

Eli shook his head and smiled, seems his wife had gotten over her fears for the moment. He also knew he was right with the discovery of gold in the mountains men were flocking to the territory from everywhere.

IT WAS MIDMORNING WHEN the men had assembled in front of the house waiting for Eli to come out. As the door opened, Eli and his wife came onto the porch, followed by Liss.

Jason smiled at Liz and tipped his hat, "Mz. Crawford."

Liz nodded and smiled at him and then smiled to all the men there. Liss looked at Jason, "morning Jason."

He smiled down at her, "morning Liss."

There was no question Melissa Gabrielle Cristina Crawford was everyone's little sister on the ranch and could get anyone of those hands to do just about anything within reason. Though she dressed like a twelve year old boy, there was no mistaken that under that cowboy hat was the prettiest chestnut red hair and one look into those eyes of her's, well one day, some man is gonna see she's a real pretty gal. But with Jason, well, that was another story, she had a special fondness for the boss man. One might even say Jason Reynolds was her knight in shining armor, why she even said one day she'd marry him.

The judge gives his daughter a hug and smiled at her, "stay out of trouble and listen to your mother."

She gave a nod as he turned to his wife, "I'll be home in a few days, stay close there's a cat out there and I'd feel safer if you and Liss stayed close." He gave her a hug and then turned to his horse and mounted up.

Liss moved near her mom as they watched Elias and the men ride out.

Jason turned once, smiled and waved to them.

Elizabeth put her arm around her daughter's shoulder, "he'll be back before you know it."

"Oh. I know Mama." With that, Liss walked back into the house.

Elizabeth has known for some time, her teenage daughter had found the foremen interesting, well, interesting as could be had from a sixteen year old girl's fantasy, the fact that Jason himself saw her as not only his boss's daughter, but just what she was a sixteen year old girl with her first crush.

IT WAS THE FIRST NIGHT of camp, Cookie had set up the chuckwagon early, just to get a head start on supper. They hoped to make it to the north pass by mid-day tomorrow. With the looks of the sky today, they seemed to be only a step away from snow falling and closing the pass.

Jason walked over to the campfire and poured himself a cup of coffee. He looked out across the night sky just hoping to get to the pass and back down before the snow. He was so occupied with his thoughts, he didn't hear Elias walk over.

"You worried Jas?"

He looked at him, "a bit Sir, you know how tricky that snowfall up on those mountains can be."

Elias shook his head, "I know, but I have a feeling we'll be alright."

"A feeling Sir?"

He smiled at him, "sure, after all I did promise the Misses that we'd be home in a week or less."

Jason smiled, he knew Liz was a bit upset being there especially with the thought of a mountain lion lurking about and well the judge wanted to ease her fears.

LIZ CARRIED THE FOOD into the dining room. It was only the first night with Elias gone and Liz already was worried.

Liss, saw the look on her mother's face, "it's alright Mama. Why I bet Papa and Jason and the men are enjoying themselves in the night air. You know they can get when they're on the trail. Why I bet they don't even miss us."

Liz looks at her daughter and smiles, she knew what she was doing. She was trying to get her mind off her father, unfortunately it wasn't working.

Liss decided to try another idea, "Mama, how old were you when you courted papa?"

Liz looked at her, "well as I recall, I was sixteen when your father invited me to my first social."

She looked at her mother, "sixteen!"

"You must understand these things are quite different back in Kansas."

She looked at her, "maybe, but sixteen Mother?"

"Well first off, your father was already four years older than I and had a profession. He was working in the lawyer's office in town and preparing to take his bar exam. Your grandfather was not in favor of him taking me to the social, but your grandmother saw no harm, after all the entire town would be there."

Liss smiled and put down her fork wanting to know more, "and you went of course."

Her mother smiled at her, "of course. I can remember the gown I wore. It was the most beautiful shade of green. Your grandmother said it brought out my eyes."

The young girl had to agree her eyes were a deep emerald green and with her hair just captured her beauty. Liss had not inherited those eyes, though they were sticking in their hazel effect with the soft green intertwined with the a touch of amber they did seem to capture the eye and interest of those who met her and her hair was the color of a warm brown with caramel and strawberry highlights scattered in the long curls. At times it was hard to believe under those jeans and flannel shirt was a young lady.

For a moment, Liz's mind took her back to that first social.

Suddenly, the sound of shots rang out. They were coming from the barn and Waco's voice could be heard telling the men to check out the other side of the barn.

Suddenly, there was a knock on the door. Waco's voice called out, "Miss Liz, I ask you and Miss Liss to stay inside until you here from me."

"Waco, is there something wrong?"

"Mz. Liz, I will let you know when I know, please stay in the house."

With that they heard footsteps leaving the porch.

Liss looks at her mom, "wonder what that is all about." She looked at her mother who was about to go into a panic, as she reached to her she placed her hands on her shoulders, "now Mama, you need to calm down. Waco and the boys have everything under control and it's best if we just come back into the main room and wait for him to come back."

She looked at her daughter, "how could she remain so calm when who knows what was happening out there?"

Liss looks at her, "Mama, just be calm."

There was the sounds of another few shots and footsteps heading toward the front door. The sound of Waco's voice called out, "Mz. Lizabeth, it's all clear now."

With that, Liz ran to the door and slowly opened it.

Waco smiled at her, "It's alright Mz Liz, sorry to put a scare into you and Liss."

Liz looked at him, "what was it Waco?"

"Well Ma'am, seems we have a small problem with a cat. I mean small, only 'bout near as I can figure ,he be interested in what was in the barn, He be just curious Ma'am, don't think he'll be back. Best we be a keeping watch near the barn for a spell. At least till the rest of the hands get back."

Liz looks at him, "yes, yes of course Waco."

He's about to leave when Liz stops him, "thank you Waco. Both Liss and I are thankful for your help."

"Waco smiled at her, "no problem Mz. Liz., we're just happy to be here to help ya." He smiles and heads back down the steps and Liz walks back into the house.

Liss looks at her, "well?"

"Seems Waco says there was a cat around the corral, he suggests we keep the horses in the barn for now or at least until more hands get back."

Liss walks over to the window and looks out toward the barn, "do you think it's safe for the filly in the barn?"

Liz looks at her, "the filly will be safe Waco is going to have one of the men stay in the tonight." She places her arm around the girl's waist and starts back into the room to sit near the fire.

As the time passed by, Liss kept wondering about the little filly and how safe she was in the barn. She knew it was silly, I mean after all, Waco had one of the hands in the barn nothing would happen to the horse.

AT THE CAMPFIRE, ELI and Jason were checking the map one more time before turning in. They both knew they had to be up before sun up and by noon, be half way into the pass.

Eli as looks at Jason, "seems if we want to get those steers out before the snow, we're gonna have to start before sunup."

Jason looks over to him then looks up to the sky. There wasn't a star in sight. "Well Sir, I hope you have a deal with The Good Lord His-self to hold off on the white stuff 'till we get back down here."

Elias looked at him. "Son, I've been asking Him that every year since we've had these trips."

Jason gave a smile to him, then slid down and rested on his saddle and began to doze off.

It was still dark when Cookie gently tugged at the judge to get up, "time to get up Judge." He hands him a cup of coffee, "this should help you get some warmth in ya."

Elias looked at him and nodded, "thanks Cookie, could sure can use this." Eli looks at Jason as he opens his eyes and slowly leans back against the saddle.

"Morning Sir. It is morning, right?"

It seemed like a normal question since it still was as dark as night around them with only the glow of the campfire to see each other by.

Elias smiles at the two men, "oh it is morning, I 'speck we have some time before the sun comes up. Mind you we have a long ride ahead of us."

Jason looks out into the darkness, he knows the trail that lays ahead, he, also, knew that they had to get through the pass, round up the steers and get back down before snow hit the high country. Didn't seem too hard until you realize they'd started this trek about two weeks later than usual and for all they know it could have already started to snow in the high country. He looked over to Elias, "Sir, you do know those steers ain't gonna move down that range unless we get there and move em."

"I'm well aware, that's why I want all of you in the saddle before I see that sun rise."

With that, Jason takes the last gulp of his coffee and grabs his saddle and heads to the remuda to his horse.

Eli looks at the others just getting up and one by one, they head toward the remuda also. He had a fine group of men working for him and his foremen was one of the best. He slowly makes his way up to Jason in the lead of the group. He admired the young men. Like himself, he had come out west to seek a new life, his only trade was his knowledge of horses and a deep passion to find that perfect stallion one day and start his own prize breed of horses. Elias perhaps saw in the young man a passion he once had. A passion that called to him to leave his law practice in Kansas and with his young wife and come to a territory that was still wild and rugged as the people who lived there. But there was something in the young man. There was no doubt he was raised with manners, why Elias couldn't remember a time he didn't call him sir or refer to Liz as Mz. Crawford. Yes, he was an excellent top hand.

Jason smiles at him as he reaches his side. "I've been a watching those clouds yonder Sir and we'd be cutting it close, but we just might make it."

Elias looks at the clouds, then back at the boy, Good Lord willing ya mean don't ya Jason?"

Jason smiles, "Good Lord willing Sir."

Elias took a deep breath and looked toward the northern ski, "take a deep breath Jason, that's telling ya there's snow coming."

Jason had known never to question the weather or law with the judge, he was an expert on both. He had come to this valley some ten years ago. A young lad ready to take on the world, when he stumbled on to the judge sitting by the banks of a creek that ran through the property. Just passing through was his goal until his met Judge Elias Crawford trying his luck on catching supper.

Eli smiled as the young man approached, "howdy."

Jason smiles and looks at the man. "Howdy Sir, had any luck?"

Eli shakes his head and smiles, "tell you the truth, seems these here fish aren't hungry. Why nary a one has even taken a nibble on my line, and mind you, I've put some fine choice worms on that line for them."

Jason smiles and slowly gets off his horse, "well, seems to me they're just down right rude. I mean here you are getting some fine food for them to enjoy and they just swim on by."

Eli looks at the boy and smiles, "you do much fishing Son?"

"Yes sir, most of the time back home, itI was eating a diet of fish daily."

"Back home, where would be?"

Jason looked down, then back up to Elias, "Missouri Sir, my folks had a small farm not too far from the river. My pa and his pa worked on the river boats 'till they got too old and settled on farming."

Elias could sympathize with the boy, he knew that working on the river was hard work and many times you were gone from your family for long periods of time. He handed the pole to Jason, "care to try your luck?"

A smile came to the boy's face as he takes the pole from Eli. "Are you sure sir?"

Eli smiled, "well I'm hoping you would have better luck."

They both smiled as Jason sat down near Elias and threw the line back in. It wasn't long before there was a tug on that line and soon after, Jason had pulled up a fine looking first course for supper.

Elias smiled, "well Son, I'd be glad to share this with ya if you would care to join me and my family at our place not far from here."

Jason looked at him, "oh Sir, that wouldn't seem fair, I mean it was your line and this is your stream..."

"Fiddlesticks, I've been sitting here all day with no luck and you just come down and sit in the very same spot and look, here's the proof. Now I'm bot hearing any no from you Son. You're coming to my ranch for supper. 'Sides, I'd like you to meet the missus and my daughter."

And with that began a friendship that turned into a bond that is still strong today. There was nothing Jason wouldn't do for the judge and Elias felt the same way about the boy. He was more than the foreman of the ranch; he was a member of the family. And so, this friendship that began with the catching of a fish is still strong fifteen years later. Elias looks over to him and smiles. Yes, he was quite satisfied with his choice to give this at the time, a job and a chance to be something.

Jason looks up at the sky then back to Elias, "Seems like the Man upstairs heard your prayers Sir."

Elias smiles and nods, "He hers everyone's prayers Son."

"Maybe so Sir, but all I know is there's the opening to the pass trail and looks like we're gonna make it there before the snow falls."

BACK HOME AT THE CIRCLE C, Liss slowly makes her way toward the barn. She made sure her mama was busy in the house and wouldn't catch her as she opened the barn door. She knows she promised her pa she wouldn't ride the filly, but she was such a sweet girl and it wasn't the first time she had ridden a horse, after all, it was her horse. Why riding a horse was as easy as walking to her. She headed toward the stall and there she stood. With the sunlight coming through the window and bouncing off her coat it looked like gold dust. She smiled and took out a cube of sugar from her pocket, and holds it out to the animal. "I knew you'd be looking for this. I have a surprise for you, we're going ridding today."

The horse looks up at her and she smiles, "yes that's right, we're going to take a tour of the ranch. But we have to be very careful. Can't let mama see us leave." Slowly she puts the blanket on the horse and then carefully she gets the saddle strapped on. The reins were the last to be placed and slowly, she opened the door of the stall and walked the horse to the barn door. Opening it, she sees there is no one around and moves forward, walking the horse. Once past the house, she gently gets on the horse and rides out slowly down the trail. Once far enough from the house, she gives the horse a gentle tug and they go off down the road. It was pure delight for Liss, the horse was responding to all the cues and it was as if they were one. With the sunlight against them, it was as if it seemed a girl and her golden horse were galloping across the countryside. They were truly a vision in gold. Maybe that's why she named her Goldie. And why not, she was a palomino and a beautiful golden one at that. Enjoying the ride so much she hardly realized she was coming up to the bend in the road. Though it was a steep turn and Liss knew the road well, the horse was not prepared for the large tree branch across the road. The horse came to a complete stop and Liss went flying form the saddle on to the dirt hitting her head on a rock and passed out. There she lay in the dirt unconscious with the horse still on the other side of the log looking at her.

Back at the ranch, Liz comes out the back door looking for her daughter when she sees Paco near the corral. "Paco, have you seen Liss?"

"No, Senora, I have not. Do you want I should look on the barn?"

"Yes, please Paco, thank you." The older man rushes to the barn door and quickly goes in. Only gone a few moments, he comes rushing out. "Senora, Senora!"

Liz stated to head toward him, "Is she there?"

"No Senora, she is not there, but the golden horse, she is gone too."

Liz knew where her daughter was now. She had disobeyed both her father's and her orders not to ride that horse until she was fully broken it. Now the question is where could she be and is she alright or lying on the road somewhere or being attacked by that wild cat with the horse running back up in the hills with the wild herd.

She looked at Paco, "Paco, please get Waco for me. I need to speak with him."

The man rushes off, "Si Senora, I will get him right now." He rushed off headed toward the bunk house.

It was only moments when Waco arrived running toward her, "Calm down, Mrs. Crawford, she can't have gone too far. I'll round up the boys."

"It's my fault, I should have watched her closely, Oh Waco, what if she's hurt and can't get to help?"

"Mrs. Crawford, just calm down, we'll find her."

Chapter 2

A young stranger makes his way up the trail; suddenly, he slows down as he sees a riderless horse just standing a few feet ahead of him. Looking around for the rider, he spots a lifeless body across the other side, near a cluster of rocks. Carefully, he gets off his horse and takes the Palomino's reins and ties her to a limb of the fallen tree limb. He then makes his way over to the injured cowboy. He was out cold, but when he turned him over, he realized it wasn't a he. What he was looking at was a young lady. who by the looks of things had been thrown from the saddle and had landed on the ground near these rocks, giving her a nasty cut on the forehead and side of her head and she was unconscious? He knew he had to get help, but there was no way he was leaving a woman alone on the trail and in the state she was in. Best he could do was try to make her comfortable and hope someone would come looking for her before dark. He took off his jacket and gently placed it under her head as he cleaned off the blood from her head wound. He looked up at the sun knowing he had a good three hours before evening would set in. He began to wonder about the girl. Wondered if she had any kin who might be looking for her. He looked at her face, she was a pretty sort. More like a young pup, on her own for the first time. Why he was even ready to bet her folks had no idea she was out here and in the state she's in.

Suddenly she began to stir, she raised her hand to her head, but kept her eyes closed. Seems she only stirred and was out again. The cowboy walked over to the larger rock and sat down, seems like he was gonna be there a spell. Taking his tobacco pouch from his pocket, he began to make himself a cigarette. Within a short time, he was enjoying a peaceful smoke, just watching the smoke float through the air. *Sure was a peaceful place* he thought, *why it's down right pretty with the stream off to the side. Yep, it's a pretty little spot, a body could maybe settle down here, then maybe again not.* He looked over at the girl still out cold, she sure was a pretty little thing. Yet, by the way she was dressed one would easily take her for a young teenage boy.

BACK AT THE RANCH, Waco and the men have saddled up and are getting ready to go and look for Liss, "don't you worry Mrs. Crawford, we'll find her."

Liz looks at him. He can see besides being angry, there was also fear in her eyes. Liss was headstrong, but she always came back before the late afternoon. Besides with that horse, no telling where she be or if she was hurt or not. He moves the men out as Liz stands on the porch until they are out of sight.

MEANWHILE, IT SEEMS Liss is starting to come around. She begins to stir and a soft moan is heard. Slowly, she reaches to her head and feels the bandana tied around it. She opens her eyes and is startled to see she is lying on the ground. She tries to sit up, but a wave of dizziness hits her and she falls gently back down.

As she touches her head again, she hears a man's voice, "I'd be real easy on getting up. You have a nasty cut on your head. Must be when you were thrown from your horse and on to them rocks."

She opens her eyes and tries to focus on the man's face, which is starting to come int focus.

He looks at her and smiles, "howdy, glad to see you're up. Like I said ,you have a nasty cut on your head and..." his voice had a smooth easy drawl not from round these parts.

Before he could continue Liss stops him, "excuse me Sir, but is it customary for a gentleman to let a lady, an injured lady to lay there and..."

Before she could stop, he walks over to her, "first off Ma'am, I didn't leave you lay there. I came up and saw your horse standing here then I saw you laying there. I saw you had a cut on your head and you was unconscious, so I tended you best I could and let you be, figuring when you came to you could let me know where you came from, so's I could help you get home."

She sat up slowly and looked at him, "Am I to believe you simply were just sitting here waiting for me to awaken to..."

A smile came to his face, "the name's Cully Ma'am. Michael Patrick Culhane Jr, folks just call me Cully."

"Well Mr. Cully."

He stops her, "just Cully Ma'am, and you might be…"

She looks at him, "the name's Liss Crawford."

He looks at her, "Liss?"

She rolls her eyes, then looks back at him, "Melissa Gabrielle Christina Crawford."

He smiles, "pleasure to meet you, Miss Crawford." His voice questions his last word as if he wondered she preferred to be a miss or does she want to be a boy…

She looks at him, "just Liss."

He smiles at her. He still had to admit she was a pretty little thing. He moves closer to her and hands her the canteen, "would you like some?"

She nods and takes the canteen from him.

"Mind if I ask you a question, Miss Crawford?"

She nods and he continues, "well, do you think you can tell me where you live, so I can get you back home? I mean, your folks may be worried and you really need some doctorin' on that cut."

She handed him back the canteen, "look Mr. Culhane."

"Cully."

"Alright Cully, I am perfectly able to get home on my own, so of ya'll don't mind, just leave me here and…"

"Oh but Ma'am, that's totally against my upbringing. Why, my mama would never think that her boy would leave a young lady, who was injured alone to get back home."

She looked at him, "listen, Country Boy, what your mama taught you is not what I need. Now if ya'll just let me get on my horse, I'll be headed back home before ya know it."

"Are you sure you can…"

She gets up on her feet, "Mr. Cully, are you always this unagreeable or is it only with women? I assure you I am capable of getting home without your help." Slowly, she makes her way toward Goldie and on to the horse.

Cully watches her as she turns and smile, "thank you for your concern, Mr. Cully." With that, she turns and slowly rides off. Cully quickly gets on his horse and follows, but at a safe distance as not to get her riled up. She sure was a stubborn one. He never did see a female so determined to refuse help, when anyone with half a mind could see she was not strong enough to ride home alone, no matter how far it would be. Speaking about far, he began to wonder how far was her folks' ranch was.

Liss began to feel a bit dizzy again, perhaps she should have taken that Cully's offer. She shook her head, that was nonsense after all, she was completely capable to get home and didn't need no stranger leading her home. Besides, what would her pa think, having some stranger take....

She suddenly blacks out and slumps against the saddle. Cully, not more than twenty feet away sees what is happening and rides up to help. He gets up to her and close enough to take the reins and secure her in the saddle with her hands on the saddle horn with the reins and takes the bridle to keep Goldie from running off. She looks up as she hears his voice, "Miss Crawford, how far are we from your ranch?"

Her voice somewhat slurred tries to say, another few miles. Suddenly, there was not only a clap of thunder, but the beginning of rain.

Cully knew he had to get her to some type of shelter, there was no way they could continue in this weather.

The rain seemed to be upon them and the trail had turned into a shallow stream in a matter of minutes. Waco and his men had no choice, but to turn back. It's not that he wanted to, but it was no use, the trail was a stream and there was a chance Liss could be at the ranch right now. He looked over to Paco, "let's get back to the ranch, maybe she's back there already."

Paco looks at him, "you sure she's there Waco?"

He looks at the man, "I'm not sure of anything, my friend, but I'm sure we can't go any farther and we can't leave Mz. Liz alone back at the ranch, especially with that cat wandering around."

The man had to agree and they turned back, followed by three more hands.

SNOW HAD BEGUN TO FALL as Elias and the men reached the opening at the pass. Lightly falling flurries seemed to be the warning that the north pasture was snow covered and it would soon head down to the lower pastures. Montana was noted for its heavy snow storms and Eli knew that his herd may have been saved from the snow, but there was still the threat of the animals searching for food.

Cookie had set up camp early as usual and hot coffee sounded just about right as Eli rode into camp and got off his horse. Cooke looked at him as he poured him his coffee, "here ya go Boss."

Eli smiled, "thanks Cookie, I tell ya, I've been thinking about this since we got down the pass. Sure does hit the spot." He took sip and smiled, "Cookie, you do make a good cup of coffee."

The old man smiled, "thank you Judge." Cookie had been with the Circle C since the judge and the missus had come to the ranch. Why Cookie, Jason, Waco and Paco were the first hands the judge hired. The judge considered them more like family than hands. They were there when Miss Lissie was born and watched her grow up. They were like the uncles she never had and there was never a doubt that they were devoted to her. Eli sat down by the fire, that northern wind was building up and it was a sure sign that snow was on its way, he could feel it in his bones. He had to admit maybe it was time he stepped down and left the roundup for the younger fellas. After all he wasn't so young anymore and Liz had been trying to talk him into staying home each year. He did miss sleeping in his bed at home something the hard dirt floor could not take its place. He also missed Liz, after twenty eight years with the woman he had to say she was worth coming home to. When they first came out west, it was a far cry from the life she had in Kansas, yet she never complained nor said she wanted to go back. She stayed with him through it all and never said a word. Yes, she was a fine woman. Lost in his thoughts, he didn't hear Jason come up beside him and sit down.

"You look like a man with the weight of the world on your mind Sir, is there anything I can do to help?"

"Oh, just thinking about the girls back home and how they're doing."

Jason knew where his thoughts were and decided maybe he should offer him a solution, "well Sir, if you want, you could head back tomorrow, you'd be at the ranch by early evening and we'll bring the heard down the next day."

The judge had to admit the offer was tempting, but he set this roundup from the start and he was determined to end it. "No, I'll end it with y'all, but I'll make this my last roundup. It's time to let you young folks do the work, besides the missus will be happy to hear this."

They both smiled and nodded. Jason, as well as the others knew Mz. Crawford usually got the judge to see her way after a bit.

He smiled at Jason, "mind you, I ain't letting her win Son, it's just, well she's a stubborn woman, but truth be told there ain't any better than her and I thank the Good Lord each day, she's by my side all these years."

Jason looked at him, "I hear ya Judge, ain't no finer woman than Mz Liz."

The judge looked at him and smiled, "Thank you, Son." There was a genuine tone to his voice he appreciated the boy's compliment. He had a fondest for Jason, maybe it was the way they met, maybe he saw in him the boy he once was. Whatever, he was glad he was a part of the Circle C and the family.

STILL TRAVELING SLOWLY in the rain and mud, Cully knew he had to find a place for Liss, not only to rest, but to dry off. Those clothes she had on were soaked to the skin. Suddenly, through the row of trees, he spotted a dim light and what looked to be a cabin. A cabin out here in nowhere seemed odd, but right now it was a miracle. He began to pick up the pace, but it still was slow going, due to the mud.

He gently took her off the horse and into his arms as he slowly makes his way to the cabin door. Gently kicking the door with his boot, he waited as the door slowly opened and an old man appeared. He opened the door wider as he invited Cully inside. "Come in, come in, I saw you down the road and hoped you saw my light. Why it's not a night for riding and from the looks of it seems you have a bit of a problem there." He looked at Liss and saw the gash on her forehead which was bleeding again. He led Cully through a nearby door and another room with a bed at the far end of the room. "You can have her lay down here. Poor young thing, she looks plumb tuckered out. You should know better than going off and getting stuck in a mess like this."

He looked at Cully and then smiled. He remembered there was a time he was young and foolish too. He smiled at Cully, "If you don't mind, I'd like to take a look at her cut. Now don't be worrying, I'm a doctor, you take a look outside the door of the cabin, my shingle is there Doctor Ben Woodward MD." A smile came to his face when he said his name. He said it with pride and conviction.

Cully looked at him, "I'd appreciate it Sir."

Slowly, Doc Woodward moved Liss' head, so he could see her wound. "that's a nasty cut, how did it happen?"

Cully looked at him, he couldn't very well tell him, since he didn't know rightly how it happened, so he invented a story. He walked over to the door, "well, we were just riding alone, it was a nice day and well, you know how it is, she decided to race me into town. I tried to tell her that horse of hers was still a bit skittish, but well, you know how women can't be told what they can't do."

The old man still working on the cut just smiles and shakes his head.

Cully continues, "well, we came across this turn and before you know it, there was this tree limb right across the road. Well, Goldie stopped short and Liss went over the horse and landed on the ground surrounded by rocks, I figure she hit her head on one of them, that's how she got that cut."

The doc looked at him, "has she been like this since she fell?"

"She's been in and out a few times, but not long enough to ride on her own."

The old man looks at the boy, "well, since she has been to a few times is a good sign. I'm not saying she's not in danger, let's see how she is in the morning."

He saw the look of relief on Cully's face, "don't worry Son, I'll take good care of your missus."

Cully looked at the old man, but wasn't about to correct him, after all, how would he explain how they were together. Cully walked over to the window, the rain was still coming down and there was no doubt they wouldn't be able to get any farther than they did. He had to admit finding this cabin was nothing short of a miracle, especially for someone who doesn't believe in such a thing. He looked back at the old man who gently placed a blanket on the girl then smiled at Cully, "I'll leave you the candle, if you need me for anything, I'll be in the other room. You'd better get some rest too and might want to get out of those wet clothes too. Can't have you both coming down with pneumonia." He smiled and closed the door as he left.

Cully walked over to the cot and looked down at Liss; she looked so peaceful. He sat down alongside the bed, took off his shirt, leaned back and closed his eyes, it didn't take long before he had drifted off to sleep also.

He was awakened by the tapping on the door. Getting up and wrapping the blanket around him, he opened the door. The old man smiled at him as he held a tray with two coffee cups on it. "Morning Son, I didn't want to wake you too early, but I thought you and the young lady could use some coffee. How's she doing?" The old man handed him the tray and walked over to Liss,

Cully followed him, "well, she seemed to have slept through the night and well, you can see for yourself, she seems better."

Doc looked up at him, "oh I see, I, also, noticed you were kind enough to let her have the bed while you slept on the floor. Now I find that a true gentleman. She's got herself a good man. That she does."

Cully smiled at the old man. He didn't like deceiving the man, but with the circumstances as they were, well, there wasn't any other choice."

The old man looked at him, "if you'd like my advice Son, as soon as she's able, I'd get her back home. I'm sure she'd feel a whole lots better in her own bed." He smiles at him. "I'm thinking you would too.'"

Cully gave him a smile and nodded. Suddenly, Liss began to stir and opened her eyes. She looked up and saw the old man smiling at her, "well it's good to see you with your eyes open Young Lady, and may I add such pretty eyes at that."

She smiled back at him and still looked a bit uneasy, so the doc filled her in.

"I suppose you have a lot of questions, but first off, I'm Doctor Benjamin Woodward and well, you and the handsome hubby of yours were caught in a bad storm last evening and well, you were just lucky to happen to come upon my cabin. You were in sorry shape with that nasty cut on your head."

She reached up and touched the bandage and he smiled, "oh not to worry, I took care of it."

She smiled at him, "thank you.'"

As the old man suspected she had a soft gentle drawl to her speech that just added to her beauty along with those hazel eyes, it was easy to see why the young fella fell in love with such a gal. Oh there was no mistake the old man wasn't too old to notice the look in a young man's eye when it's love, and there was no mistake that young man loved his lady. He smiled at her and got up, "well, I'll give you two some privacy, I'll let you know when breakfast is ready." He headed for the door and was gone.

She looked at Cully, "you told him I was your wife?"

Cully moved toward her.

"You keep your distance! The nerve of you telling such a lie! I should have you horse whipped, I, should,'" she stopped when she suddenly noticed she had no clothes on.

He moved closer to her, "just keep your voice down. Look you were in no shape to keep traveling, the rain was making it impossible to go on. By luck, I saw this cabin and well, I took a chance. When the good doctor opened the door and saw you out cold in my arms."

She looks at him, "you had me in your arms?"

He stopped and looked at her, "can I please finish the story?"

"Oh by all means, but let me get this straight, I was in your arms?"

He looked at her, "you were out cold, how was I supposed to get you in the cabin?"

She nods, "true, but you had…"

He didn't let her finish, "I can see this is a problem for you, so when you can understand I did nothing wrong, we'll end this conversation."

She saw she had pushed the matter too far and looked at him, she did like the fact she could get him riled up easy. "I'm sorry, so how do we tell the man he made a mistake?"

"Well, I was thinking, why tell him anything. Let him think what he thinks and in the morning; we go on our way and a mile down the road, split up and go our separate ways."

"You mean to spend the night here!"

"Look, we can either carry on this little white lie or make this old men unhappy. You saw the way he smiled when he spoke about his wife. Come on. don't you have any feelings?"

She looked at him and for the moment he actually saw her. Saw the woman she tried so hard to hide. Those hazel eyes that had just the right touch of green to make them capture a man's soul and hold it. Her brown hair with just a touch of red and gold that seemed to set off her soft light skin that she had tried to hide with that cowboy hat all this time. Oh there was no mistake she was a woman and a beautiful woman, and if she tried could be a very desirable woman. Here he had thought she was just a child. Goes to prove always take a second look.

She noticed him too, those clear blue eyes and that hair, the color of a raven wing, oh she did notice him, maybe a bit more than she should have, but this, what they had here was not the time or place to start something that could never go any farther. He was a total stranger and …"

He looked at her, he had to admit it was wrong not to tell Doc the truth, but in honesty, he didn't want to hurt the old man's feelings and most of all he wanted to stay with her.

Suddenly, there was a light tapping on the door and Cully opened the door. "Hey Doc, we were just getting ready to join you for breakfast," he looks at Liss. "wasn't that right Dear?"

She smiles at both of them. "We sure were, I'm famished Doc, hope you have plenty of coffee to go with breakfast." She puts her arm in Doc's as they walk toward the table, she turns and looks back at Cully and smiles.

He had to admit she was a beautiful woman he just couldn't understand how he missed it all this time.

Sitting at the table, Liss smiles at the doc, "this was all so sweet of you Doc," she looked over at Cully, "isn't this sweet of the Doc Honey?" showing off her southern drawl.

It was a peaceful breakfast and she seemed to enjoy keeping ole Doc Woodward in a happy mood.

Cully knew this all would have to come to an end soon. He was sure Liss's folks would be out looking for her.

Doc Woodward looked at Cully who seemed to be miles away in thought, "Cully, you seem lost in your thoughts Son, is everything alrighty?"

Cully looked at the old man, "I was just thinking how this has been a real treat for you as well as us Doc. After all, you yourself said hardly anyone comes his way."

The old man nods, "true, why it's as if you were sent to me, it's as if the Lord wanted us together."

Liss looked at them and smiled, "well, it's settled, we have to come see Doc once a week from now on."

"Well, I didn't mean that you young'uns..."

She taps his hand with hers, "now Doc, we will not hear anything like that," she looks over to Cully, "isn't that right Honey?" There was a twinkle in her eyes. A twinkle he couldn't say no to. *How in his right mind could he think he was in love with a woman he had only known one day? Only one day? It doesn't happen like that. Or does it?*

The old man looks at him, "Son, you seem a bit confused?"

He looked back at the doc, "no Doc. I'm still a bit tired, I didn't sleep too well last night."

The old man nodded thinking he must have been uncomfortable on the floor while his wife was on the bed.

Chapter 4

They said their good byes to Doc and slowly made it down the trail. Liss only turned once to smile and wave to the old man, then continued until they saw neither the old men nor the cabin. Not too far off, they came across the opening to the main road just as Doc has said they would.

Cully looks over at Liss, "well, looks like this is where we part."

She didn't raise her head, she didn't want to say good bye. Call it silly, even crazy, but being with Cully and Doc last evening was the first time she felt so alive. She felt like she belonged. How could something so strange feel so right? How could a total stranger make her want to stay by his side and never go back to the life she knew. There was no way she could ever go back to the docs no way he would see the young couple he took in from the rain. She turns to Cully holding back the tears in her eyes, "I guess it is. I want to thank you for everything Mr. Cully."

"It was my pleasure Mz. Crawford. You be careful with Goldie now."

He gave her a smile and she smiled back, "I will."

He leaned over in the saddle and gave her a kiss on the cheek, "you take care pretty one." With that he rides off leaving her alone just watching him ride off.

She cupped her cheek where he had kissed her, still I shock. He called her pretty one. No one had ever besides the family have ever said she was pretty. No one ever noticed but him and now he was gone.

Cully himself was doing a bit of thinking. He just couldn't seem to get his mind off Liss. Oh he had to admit she wasn't like other gals, matter of fact, she was like no other gal he'd ever known. He knew she'd be alright, why her folks were probably with her by now.

Liss slowly made her way on the trial in no hurry to make it back to the ranch. Lost in her thoughts, she didn't hear Waco and the boys as they rode up to her, she sees a smile and a look of relief on Waco's face as he rides up to her.

"MISS LISS, WHERE IN the blazes have you been? Why you had us all worried sick."

She smiled at him, "well ya see, I went for a ride on Goldie and well ..."

Waco notices the bandage on her head, "and let me guess, she throwed ya."

She smiled at him, "why yes, yes, she did and well..."

He looked at her again, "and you want to tell me who bandaged your head and where you spent the night and..."

She stopped him, "well if'in you'd give me a chance I will tell you."

He smiles at her, he wasn't sure to be happy to see her all right or mad at her for riding off on that horse. "Well, I'm waiting to her your story."

She looks at him and begins, "well, you already know I took Goldie out of her stall and decided it was such a nice day and well, you know ... Well, I just had to ride her and she wanted to run, I could feel it. We took off down the road and I knew Mama would be upset, but we were having such a good run and then it happened."

Waco looked at her, "what happened?"

"There was a tree limb in the road, why it stretched across the whole road. It took poor Goldie by surprise. Well, she came to a full stop and I went over her and landed across on the ground near a pile of rocks."

He looks at her, "and the horse bandaged your head?"

She touches her head. "Well of course not." She knew she would have to explain something she was trying hard to avoid. "Well you see, I was. I was lying there on the side of the road when this gentleman came riding up. He saw Goldie just standing there and saw me trying to get up."

Waco looked at her, "you mean to tell me a total stranger....?"

"Now Waco, don't ya go making somethin that it weren't. He was a fine gentleman and ...well, hells bells, he thought I was a boy at first."

The men started laughing at that remark and Waco looks at them and then looks back at Liss. "Well, this fella comes along and..?"

Liss looks at him and realizes the story begins to sound a bit crazy even for her. "Well, he cleaned up the cut best he could and offered to help me get home when the rain started. Well, we had been riding along when he saw this cabin. It's back there a bit, I can take you..." she stopped when she realized if she went back there, how would she explain all these men to Doc. He was under the impression that her and Cully were newlyweds."

Waco looked at her, "you were saying you saw this cabin back there and ..."

Suddenly, a rider was galloping their way. When Liss looked up she saw it was Cully. She was almost in disbelief, why was he coming back, why now? He slowed his horse down and came to a gentle halt when he got to them.

He smiled as Liss. "I see your family found you, I was hoping I would find they had."

Waco looked at him, "I suppose you're the good Samaritan who helped her when the horse threw her."

Cully looks at him and offers his hand to him, "Michael Patrick Cullhane, Sir, but everyone calls me Cully."

Waco shakes his hand, "well, Mr. Cully, I want to thank you for your kindness to Liss and I know her mother would like to thank you personally. If you care to ride along with us back to the Circle C, you could meet her."

Cully smiles at him then looks over at Liss, "I'd be happy to."

Waco looks at Liss, "well, let's get back home."

They slowly ride off with Cully riding alongside of Liss, who is keeping her head down. With Waco ahead of them, Cully was at least able to talk to her, but it was Liss who started the conversation. "Why did you come back?"

He smiled at her, "well, to tell the truth, I was kinda worried about you. Why I still don't know."

She shot him a look and he smiled, "always get you riled up, don't I?"

"You still didn't answer me."

"I came back 'cause I was worried."

"Worried about me? I never ...."

"Well, maybe someone should start worrying about you. Tell me how did you explain where we spent the night?"

Still waiting for her to answer when he fires another question at her, "I'm sure that explanation was interesting. Oh yes, did you also mention the doc or did you plan on taking them back there to meet him? Oh yes, can't do that since the old boy thinks we are married."

She looked at him. Oh, how she wished she had a gun right now, she'd shoot him right betwixt the eyes.

Cully looked at her, those witchy eyes of hers staring intently at him. He knew she was planning something in that mind of hers, just what he was afeared to ask, "You keep looking at me like that and maybe I'll tell these folks about our night in the cabin."

She looked at him, "you hush your mouth and don't you be a saying another word."

IT WAS ABOUT NOON WHEN Elias and the herd were in the south pasture. They had made good time and except for that light snow at the pass, they made it down and on to lower ground in good time. He sat on his horse and looked over the steers as they moved by. Yep, they would bring a good price maybe even a bit extra to send Liz and Liss on a trip back east for a vacation. He had promised his Liz all these years they'd go back one day for a visit but the time never came and now that Liss was all grown up well...

Jason slowly made his way beside the judge. "Well Sir, seems you've got a fine lookin herd again. Should bring a good price."

"I was thinking the same myself Son. Maybe enough to send the girls back east for a trip.'"

"Well you know Mz. Liz would like that, but don't rightly know about Liss."

"I know what you're saying, but it's time she learned she's a lady, not a ranch hand."

Jason smiled, "well Sir, you and I know that, but is someone gonna tell Mz Liss that?"

The judge looked at him and smiled, he knew exactly what he meant. As long as he knew her no one was ever able to convince Liss she just wasn't one of the guys, she was a gal. Heck, when he first saw her, he thought she was boy. It's just plumb unnatural for a gal as pretty as her to hide herself in men's clothes and act like a ranch hand. But like the judge said, "one day s he'll find something or someone that will make her see differently and Lord help us, we'll have a female to deal with."

IT WAS LATE AFTERNOON when Waco, Liss, Cully and the gang headed back to the ranch. Standing on the front porch was Liz waiting. As she sees them approach, Liss can see even at a distance the look on her face. Somehow, she knew she was in for one of those dreaded long talks.

Waco rides up ahead figuring it best to tell her who the stranger was.

Cully looks over to Liss and for the first time sees the look of fear on her face. The young girl who was a feared of no one had the look of fear on her face as she looked at the woman on the porch.

Waco gets off his horse as Liz greets him. "I see you found her and I bet she has some wild excuse this time."

"Well tell ya the truth Ma'am, she was in a bit of an accident."

Liz was about to get down from the porch when Waco stopped her, "Now Ma'am, this time I tells ya, it wasn't her fault. Well, you see she was riding along on Goldie when they came across a large tree limb. Well, you see Goldie got a bit spooked and well, she came to a stop and Miss Liss, she went over the horse and landed in this pile of rocks. That's how she got that gash on her head."

Liz looks at Cully and then back to Waco, "and the young man who is with you?"

Waco knew he'd have to explain Cully, "well, Mz Crawford, he was the one who found Miss Liss and helped her."

Liz looked at Waco, "and where did they spend the night? Or did he have a place of shelter in his saddle bags?"

"No Ma'am Miss Liss told us she was heading back here when the storm hit, they found a cabin not too far off the trail and a gentleman offered them a place to stay until the rain stopped."

Liz looked at Waco, "and you believed that story?"

Waco looked at her, "yes Ma'am I do, I never saw any reason for Miss Liss not to tell me the truth.'"

Cully gets off his horse, then walks beside Liss as he helps her down and taking her arm, he helps her up the three steps on the front porch. As they get closer to Liz, the expression on her face changes to a smile to greet the young man. As she extends her hand to Cully, "welcome to the circle C, I'm Elizabeth Crawford."

Cully extends his hand and smiles at her, "pleasure to meet you Mz. Crawford, and I apologize for showing up unexpectantly here."

"Don't be silly, Waco told me you helped my daughter and for that, I thank you." Liz looks at Liss and then back to Cully, "and for that. I insist you stay with us for supper."

They followed her in the house and Liz leads them into the pallor. "Do sit down Mr. Cully, can I offer you something to drink? Coffee, tea, lemonade?"

Liss looked at her, "Mama, I think we've taken up enough of Mr. Cully's time."

Cully looks at her, he was content sitting there and was rather enjoying the conversation with Mrs. Crawford.

Liz looks at her, "I find that very rude of you Dear, after all the man did help you," she turns to Cully and smiles, "so tell me Mr. Cully. Waco said you found a cabin last night in the rain."

Cully looks at Liss, then back to Liz, "yes, well, we had started on the trail when the rain was getting heavier, with Liss's cut on her head and the loss of blood, she was just too weak to go on. It was then I saw the dim light from the window of a cabin not too far ahead. So I made our way up to the cabin and this nice gentleman, Doctor Woodward took us in and after he patched up Liss's head, he insisted we stay until morning and well..."

Liz looked at him, "I see, and where did you stay the night?"

Liss looked at her mother, "Mother, what do you think?"

Cully looked at both of them, "I don't know what you think Mz Crawford, but I can tell you your daughter was perfectly safe. Why we can go back to the cabin and Doc Woodward will tell you just what I told you."

Liz seemed to accept Cully's answer and they continued pleasant conversation.

ON THE SOUTH RANGE the drovers would be getting ready to bed down the herd for the night. As the drovers watched over the steers, the howling of the wolves could be heard in the far off distance getting closer.

Elias looks out across the range, it was a beautiful sight, but he had to admit he had to agree with Liz this could possibly be his last roundup. Maybe Liz was right. He had to admit she was right most of the time, though he wouldn't admit it. But the open sky and cold nights were not as pleasant as they were years ago.

He missed the comfort of a feather bed and the warmth of walls around him. He had to admit though they had made good time and got down through the pass before the snow began. He walked over to the campfire and sat against a large boulder, he looked at the flames so deep in thought he didn't hear Jason come up beside him until he sat down.

"You seem a bit lost in your thoughts Sir."

He turned and smiled at the boy, "well Jason, I've been thinking is gonna be my last roundup."

he boy looked at him, "last one Sir?"

"Yep, I'm figuring this is too much for a man my age. You know I'm not as young as I was ten years ago. Hell, I'm not as young as I was five years ago." He started to chuckle, "so I was thinking of making you in charge from now on."

Jason looked at him, "in charge..."

Before he could finish the sentence, Elias continues, "I know you can do it Son, it would mean a lot of worry off of me and you know the missis will be happy I will be home more."

Jason looked at him, "if that's what you want Sir."

Elias pats his back, "it's what I want Son." He looks at Cookie, let's have some of that stew you been bragging about."

Just then a young drover came riding in the camp at a fast pace. He jumped off his horse and raced over to Jason and Elias. "Mr. Jason, they sent me here to fetch you!" The poor boy was completely out of breath as he looked at Jason. "Wolves, they came down from the hills, the steers are getting ...." He gasped for a breath of air, but Jason was already on his horse and riding out. The boy tried to get up to follow, but Elias held on to him. "Sit right down Son and catch your breath. Jason will handle it." He looks at Cookie, "Cookie get this young man something to drink and let's try some of that stew you've been bragging about." He looked back at the boy, "what's your name Son?"

"Lucas Sir, Lucas Mullins."

"Well Lucas Mullins, all I want you to do right now is to sit here and have supper with me. Would you like that?"

A smile came to the boy's face, "yes sir, thank you Sir."

Cookie hands the boy a tin plate of stew and one for the judge.

Elias looks at the boy, "well. I'm ahead Son, enjoy."

The boy takes a mouthful and a smile comes to his face. He takes another mouthful and smiles up at the judge, "Judge, Sir, I'm meaning no disrespect to Mr. Cookie, but this here stew is my mama's recipe."

"Are you sure Son?"

"Yes sir, Judge, these here be the same sourdough biscuits my mama would put in her stew. Sure does take me back to memories of home."

Elias looks at the boy. Why he couldn't be no more than seventeen himself and out on his own. "Where's home Son?"

Lucas looked at him, "Missouri Sir. My pa and grandpa have a small farm not far from Collier, it be just a dot on the map as my pa always said. Ya see my grandma, she was the daughter of a Spanish noble fella and well, when she married my grandpa, he promised he wouldn't take her away from her follks, so they settled on the land close to her folks."

Elias listened to the boy and smiled, "how many of you Mulins, are there?"

The boy looks at the judge, "well Sir. twicks my mamma. Pa and Grandpa, they'd be four boys countin' me and three sisters."

Elias sat there trying to figure a way to get the family here. "Tell me something Lucas, would your family like to come out here to Montana? I can offer them good jobs and a place to live?"

"I can't rightly say Sir, but I can ask 'em."

Elias smiled, "well, why don't you go and relax, get yourself some rest, we'll talk in the morning."

The boy got up, smiled and started over toward the saddle blankets still carrying the tin plate.

Cookie looked at the judge, "Judge Sir, you gonna take that boy's family out here?"

Elias looked at him, "I was considering it, why?"

"Well, I think that's mighty nice of you, mighty nice."

Elias looked at him, "well, I'm glad you approve Cookie. By the way, you make sure to give this recipe to the missus, it's very good."

Cookie smiles. "yes sir Judge, yes sir."

Chapter 5

Back at the Circle C, Liss is making her way down the stairs and into the pallor where Liz is keeping Cully entertained. From the hall, Liss could hear Liz's voice, "So you said you just happened to ride up along the trail when you came up on my daughter lying in the dirt.'"

He looked at her, "yes, as I told Waco, I had come along when I noticed the horse, then looked over and saw she was trying to get up. I noticed the cut on her head and offered to help get her home if she would tell me the direction. She tried to get up, but she was still very unsteady on her feet."

Liz seemed to accept that answer for the moment, but Cully had the feeling this interrogation was far from over. "I see, now the question of where you both spent the night. and she empathized both.

Cully did not like what she was imposing or trying to get him to say and would not fall into her game of cat and mouse. He looked at her, not seeing Liss in the doorway of the room, "as I told Waco, we started for the direction of your ranch, when the rain started. It didn't take long afore it was coming down so hard the trail was turning into a stream. Miss Liss, she was getting unsteady in the saddle, I knew I had to find shelter for her soon. By some miracle off to the right I saw the light of a cabin and I headed towards it. A nice old man Dr. Woodward greeted us at the door and took us in. He was kind enough to tend to Miss Crawford's wound and let her spend the night in the bedroom while both he and I were in the other room, sitting by the fire."

Liz looks at him, "And how did you explain yourselves to the doctor?"

This is where Cully had to lie, but it was for a good reason. "I told him we were riding and she fell from her horse." He looked at Liz, her eyes searching to find anything in his story that she could find a lie.

Suddenly, Liss came in the room, "Mother, how could you? Mr. Cully was kind enough to help me and you're turning a simple act of kindness into something… I just can't believe you would even think."

Liz looks at Cully, "you must forgive my daughter Mr. Cully, she's well she's never been with a man before and well, you understand a mother's concern."

Cully gave her a half-hearted smile, "no need to explain, and I can understand your questions, you have a beautiful daughter and one day she'll see that."

Liz smiled, she had to admit with such manners in this frontier is a pleasant change.

Cully arises and walks over to Liz, "I thank you for a lovely evening, Mrs. Crawford, I don't know how long it's been since I've had the honor of dinning with two lovely ladies." He takes Liz's hand and with all the gallantry of a fine southern gentleman, "Mrs. Crawford, I was touched by your kindness." He gently kisses her hand, then turns to Liss, he takes her hand and looks into her eyes, "Miss Crawford, it's been a pleasure to be of service to you."

She smiles as he gently kisses her hand.

BACK AT THE CAMP, THE men were relaxing in the spare time with a friendly game of poker. The big winner of the evening so far, was a drover named Walker. He seemed a regular fella he had signed up for the roundup, said he had done this sort of work in the past, basically he was a drifter, but so were many who signed on in the past. Some stayed and made the Circle C home, others, well they moved to the next job. Most of 'em never really taken roots.

Not many were like Jason. There was a kind of loyalty, a respect the boy had for the man.

Elias knew the boy would move heaven and earth if he asked him to. Elias smiled a`s he walked past the small circle of drovers playing cards. Elias smiled at the boys, "well, who's the big winner here so far?"

"Walker, Sir seems he's got lady luck sitting on his shoulder tonight."

Elias smiles and moves on.

Jason gets up, "if you men don't mind, I'll call it a night while I still have a few dollars in my pocket."

Walker looks at him, "what's the matter Trail Boss, too chicken to try to win your money back?"

He looks at Walker. True he never did like the man, but as long as he did a day's work, he let his attitude slip by, but they were at the end of the trail now and tomorrow he'd pay him off and never have to see him again. "Walker, you have been lucky tonight, don't press your luck."

Walker looks at him, "is that an order Mr. Bossman?"

"Take it any way you want to."

"Well then, I quit. I'll be taking my wages now and head out."

Jason looks at him, "you can leave, but you'll get your wages tomorrow like everyone else, when we get back to the ranch."

The man looked at him and smiled, "alright, I'll leave, but I'll be at the ranch in the morning and I'll be expecting my money."

He walks off and Jason moves over to the judge, "I can't say I'm sorry to see him go, there was just something ..."

Elias looked at him, "I know what you mean, I wasn't sure about him either."

"And you didn't..."

Before Jason could finish, Elias looks at him, "so we needed every man we could get to get that herd down. You know yourself, most of these men will leave after tomorrow with the exception of two or three, it's a thing we face each year." He put his hand on Jason's shoulder, "by the way, that young boy Lucas Mullins, I want you to send word to his folks and see if they'd be coming out here."

"Sir?"

"Just send the wire Jason, I'd like to do something for the boy's folks."

Jason didn't question the judge. He knew from years of working for him, he usually had good reasons for his actions and if he wanted that wire sent to the boy's family, he'd make sure it got to them as soon as the sun came up that morning.

Elias walked over to the campfire and poured hisshelf a cup of coffee as Cookie walks over to him, "can I get ya anything Judge?"

He looked over at him. "No. Thanks, just a cup of coffee will do." He moved from the fire and looked out in the darkness where the steers were. It was a quiet night, one where all you could hear was the soft bellowing of the herd. They were content now they were on Circle C land and in a few weeks, they'd be on their way to the train yards. Eli smiled, he knew tomorrow night, he could sit back and relax in his study, knowing his days of roundups were over. He was glad about it, it was time he relax and do things with Liz, she had been wanting him to go with her and Liss back east for a visit. Besides, as Liz put it, one day it would be just him and Liss. Elias thought about that too. He pictured his seventeen year old daughter who was more at home in jeans and a flannel shirt than a fancy dress. Why, half the boys in the county didn't know she even existed and those who did, she at one time or another whipped the tar out of 'em. Lost in his thoughts he didn't hear Walker standing behind him with his gun drawn on him and a smiled on his face.

"What can I do for you Son?"

Walker looked at him. "first off, I ain't your son, old man."

Elias looked at him, "okay, you've made your point. What do you want?"

"Well you see Old Man, I believe I have wages coming to me. Wages I earned and want."

Elias looked at him, "well, there's no denying on the wages, and tomorrow when we reach the ranch, all of you will be paid off."

Walker not amused, "well, you see there's the problem Old Man, I don't want to wait. Now I'll just take my wages now and whatever extra you happen to have."

Elias smiles, "well Son, you're not going to happy at all. I've only a twenty dollar gold piece in my vest pocket. It's more a good luck charm than money. You're welcomed to it. Take it and ride off and no one needs to get hurt."

Walker looks at the man, "how do I know this is all you have? I mean you 'spect me to think a fancy man like you has no money on him, but a twenty dollar gold piece?"

Elias smiles at him. "Well, guess you have to take my word on it Son."

Again Walker gets angry. "How many times Old Man do I have to tell you, I'm not your son!"

"That's true, I apologize."

What Walker didn't realize was Cookie had slowly managed to get behind him and had his shotgun pointed at him. "Seems you pa didn't teach you no manners Boy, and you'd never pull a gun on a man without making sure there's no one behind you." It's then he hears the hammer pull back. The look of fright was on his face as he realizes that he no longer has the advantage. He turns and fires, hitting Cookie's shoulder, causing him to drop the gun as he turns, he aims again at the judge, who at this time has his gun drawn.

"I see the tables are turned a bit now, but I'm offering you the same deal. Take the twenty dollar piece and ride out of here and we'll call it even."

He looks him, "and if I don't?"

Elias smiles, "you really don't want to know."

Cookie's voice is heard, "shoot him Judge, shoott him!"

Walker looks at Elias, "I don't think you have the guts Judge."

With that remark, Elias fires and shoots the gun out of Walker's hand, "now you were saying... Look son and I use that word for use of another, pick up that gold piece and get on your horse and ride off."

Walker picks up the coin and his gun and walks into the darkness to get his horse.

"Oh one more thing Son, if I ever catch you on or near my ranch, I'll put a bullet right through that head of yours." He tuns and walks over to Cookie. "Judge, you took a big chance he wouldn't kill you."

Elias looks at him, "he 'wouldn't, it's not his way. He's the guy who would pick on a woman, not a man."

THE SUN WAS SLOWLY coming up and Liz was busy in the kitchen, making breakfast. It wasn't the usual breakfast, but it wasn't a usual day, they had a guest for breakfast. Usually, breakfast was eggs and toast, but this was Liz's way of sending the young man off on his way. After all, he did care for Liss when she was thrown from Goldie. Liss made her way down the stairs and into the kitchen. "Morning Mama."

Liz looked at her daughter, "well, you seem to be happy his morning."

"Why shouldn't I be?"

Liz looks her, she remembered how last night the girl was hanging on every word the young man was saying. True, he was interesting and quite handsome in his own way, but he was a stranger. Perhaps if Elias was here... Oh, but then again, he was too involved with his roundup to worry about his family. Family being his young and impressionable sixteen year old daughter. At times she wondered did he ever really care for either of them. She looked at her, "why don't you go and tell Mr. Cully breakfast is just about ready."

Liss shrugs her shoulders and heads out the door and toward the stairs.

Outside behind the barn, the figure of a person is crouching behind the barrel to avoid being seen. He needed to get into the house and in the judge's study. He knew he had a strong box there and it had money in it. After all, he was going to pay the hands off when they got in today. He had seen the box some months back when he had to give a package to the judge. He walked in as he was closing the box and about to put it away. He knew there was money and he was going to get it.

Inside, Liss had reached the top of the stairs and paused at the door of the room Cully was in. Gently, she taps on the door and Cully's voice is heard.

"Come in."

Slowly opening the door, Lisa smiles at him. "Mama sent me up here to tell you breakfast is almost ready."

"Well, can't miss breakfast." He gives her a smile, but he sees something in her eyes. Granted, he's only known her a short time, but it these few days he's grown to have feelings for her. Feelings that not even he could understand. Here he was feeling, well, he really didn't know what he was feeling for this young girl who he only met a few days ago. He watches her turn and head down the stairs only to stop and look to see if he was following.

Liz had the table set as they walked into the room. While she was in the dining room, Walker had managed to get into the house by the back door and was standing near the door.

Cully and Liss walked in and began to sit down,

"I'll just get the coffee, Mr. Cully, do start without me."

Liz pulsed open the door and Walker grabbed her and cupped his hand over her mouth to muffle any sound. He whispered in her ear behind her, "now, if you want to see your girl out there, I suggest you be real quiet. Ya hear me?"

Liz too terrified to say a word, just nodded her head yes.

Walker smiled and loosened his hand from her mouth, "that shows you are a smart woman Mz. Crawford."

Liz sees the bandana around his hand, "you're hurt, let me help…"

Walker pulls her over to the table and sits her roughly in the chair, "make no mistake Ma'am, I'm here for one thing, I want the money."

"Money?"

"Now don't go play all innocent on me. I know you know the old man has it stashed in his study. Now the right thing to do is just take me to it and I'll be on my way and you and that pretty gal of yours are safe."

Liss began to wonder what was taking her ma so long. "Mama? You be needing some help?"

Liz looks at Walker, "you best tell her everything's alright Ma'am."

"It's fine Dear, just getting the coffee ready."

Liss looked at Cully, "After you get to Fort Bennett, do you plan on going anywhere else in particular."

Cully looks up at her, "tell ya the truth, I didn't give it much thought. I did hear California is a nice place.'"

She looks at him, "oh, so you really haven't any plans."

He smiles at her, "no, I don't have any plans.'"

A smile comes to her face as she takes a bite of her toast. The door to the kitchen opens and Liz comes out with Walker behind her, his gun aimed at her head.

Liss gasps.

Walker looks at Cully who's hand slowly moves toward his gun. "I wouldn't get too close to that gun Boy. Not if'in you don't want to see this lady of the house's skull scattered all over this here room now."

Cully moves his hand, and Walker smiles, "well, that shows you is a smart boy, now if you would do me the honor of taking off that gun belt and throw the belt and gun over here by me, I would take it kindly."

Cully obliges the man and tosses the gun his way,

Walker smiles, "now I'll be beholding to both of you if you would kindly walk back to the table and set down in your chairs."

Liss looks at him, "why are you doing this?"

Walker looks at her, "well Miss, it be simple, I want what's due to me for the roundup and well, I figured I deserve a bit more too."

"A bit more?"

He smiles at her, "well being as how your daddy was down-right unhospitable about giving me my earnings, I think I'll just take it all."

Liss looks at him. "Why, that's stealing!"

Walker looks at her and smiles, she sure was a right pretty gal he had to admit. "You'd be right at that Miss. Sure do have to admit you're sure is fine looking young gal." He gently bushes her hair with his good hand and Cully lunges at him and Walker hits him over the head with his gun sending Cully to the floor. He looks at the ladies, "seems we have us a real hero here." He looks down at Cully who is out cold, "he ain't too bright though. be he?" He looks at Liss, "now girlie; you just get some rope from those curtains and Mz Crawford, you set yourself down in this here chair while this pretty gal ties you up."

Liz looks at him in defiance, "and if I don't?"

Walker looks at her, "now Mz. Crawford, you don't want to see me when I'm riled. You most assuredly don't want to."

Chapter 6

Slowly, Elias and his men were making their way back to the Circle C. Little did they know what was waiting for them back home.

Jason had tried to patch Cookie up, to at least drive the chuck wagon.

Elias well they all knew he would get attention when he got home. Elias was like a big ole bear, he would let Walker git away with what he did to cookie, he'd get him, but on his terms.

Jason rode up beside him, "well Sir, we should be nearing the Morgan place soon.

Elias smiles at him, "I tell you Son, I can almost taste a home cooked meal from Liz. Can't tell how much I've missed her cooking."

Jason smiled and shook his head. Oh he may have missed Liz's cooking, but Jason knew he missed being home. He could fool some of the hands, but those who have been with him all these years knew he was tired. He had been doing this for more years than he wanted to remember and well he had thought by this time well... He looks at Jason and smiles, "well Son, looks like this time next year, you'll be the boss."

"I hope I can do a good job for you Sir."

"I never had a doubt Son, never a doubt at all."

"You really believe that don't you Sir?"

"Son I've known that since the moment I set eyes on you, why I saw in you the makings of a fine young man. That's why I hired you."

At times. Jason wondered whether to believe him or not and this was one of those times. "Judge, Sir, you're just funning me."

Elias looks at the boy. "Let me tell you something Boy, I made a livin reading people's faces. Many a time it was my word if'in a body was guilty or not, whether they lived or not. Now when I tell you I saw the makin's of a fine young man, you can bet your last dollar I meant it. I knew with the right help you could be somebody in this world, and now look at you, why who would have believed it that day at the stream you'd become my foreman."

A smile comes to Jason's face as the two continue on their trail back to the Circle C.

Elias had his mind on his girls and how they would be busy getting the house ready for the party. Why the was the social event of the year where the judge opened his home to his ranch hands and neighbors where all could relax after the roundup.

Suddenly, the sound of a snap and the wheel of the Chuckwagon wanders off to the side and the wagon tilts to the side and falls, trapping Cookie under it.

The man's screams for help sent not only the ranch hands, but Jason and Elias to the wreck.

Jason the first to get to him and smiles up, "he's not hurt Sir, just pinned down. If we can move this wagon, I can pull him out." He grabs the man's arm gently and pulls him from under the wagon. He was lucky, he only was pinned under, but not hurt.

Cookie looked at Elias, "Judge Sir, I'm thinking it's time I start thinking about staying home next year. I'm getting too old and slow. Why, I shoulda seen that wheel needed fixing afore we left the ranch. I tell you..."

Before he could continue, Elias stopped him, "Cookie, you know as well as I do the wheel could have gone off at any time, even if we was still at the ranch. But if you want, I'll take your request into consideration. But mind you Cookie, I always relied on you to keep these young cowboys in line. Why, you were my right hand man out here." Elias smiles as he sees Cookie smile at him.

"Well Judge, if'in you needs me, I suppose I can stick it out a bit longer."

Elias pats his shoulder, "I'm glad you agree on that Cookie, like I said you are my right hand."

BACK AT THE CIRCLE C in the dining room tied to the three chairs are Cully, Liss and Liz.

Across the hall in the judge's study. Walker was ransacking the study. The sounds of books falling on the floor, and porcelain objects breaking led Liz to believe he still had not found the strong box.

Cully kept watching Liz and Liss, he wanted to make sure they did nothing to get Walker angry.

Meanwhile, he's busy trying to untie his hands from behind the chair. If he could get his hands free, he could get the women to safety out of the house.

Waco and the men were on the south ridge mending fence, it wouldn't be 'till late afternoon before they got here. He looked over and saw Liss had slowly moved her chair closer to the doorway by inching it across the floor and closer to Cully's hand gun that was sitting on the cabinet near the door. If she could free her hands and get the gun, she could at least change the tables, so to speak. She began to move the chair back and forth not seeing Walker had made his way back in the room hearing the muffled sound of the chair.

Cully was about to warn her when Walker grabs her by the hair and pulls her up, so she is standing, but still tied to the chair. Taking the gun, he holds it in front of Liss, "so you want the gun, do you? Well little lady, I be giving you the gun." He proceeds to empty the bullets from the gun and the bullets fall to the floor and he smiles. "Now if any of you people feel they need any use for this here unloaded gun well... He pulls Liss closer to him and looked into her eyes, "ya know something Gal, you sure is a good looker. What ya say you come with me, I can make a very nice life for a pretty thing like you."

It was Liz who spoke first, "you keep your filthy hands off my daughter!"

Walker looks over to Liz, "well now is it you be feeling a bit jealous Ma'am? Well tell ya. I'd be willing to take both of you with me when I leave here, yes sir, I can show you both a fine time." He pulls Liss toward him and kisses her cheek.

Liss spit in his face.

"Why you," Walker slaps her on the side of her face.

Yet Liss only looks at him and smiles, "is that your best shot? Heck, I've had better smacks from a cow's tail at milking time."

He goes to slap her again only Cully who had freed his hands, leaps on him. Both men scramble to the ground.

Liss continues to try to free her hands and when she finally does, she runs to her mother and frees her hands, then grabs Walker's gun. Aiming it on both of them, "gentlemen, if you please!"

Cully looks at her and pulls Walker up from the floor. He walks toward Liss who is still holding the gun on Walker and gently takes it from her. "Miss Liss, if you'd be kind enough to give me the gun, I'd feel a bit more comfortable if you weren't holding it."

She looked at him, "Why?"

"Well for one very good reason, you've got the one with no bullets."

She looks at the gun and Walker makes a run for the door only to be shot in the leg by Liz who had gotten the shotgun from the mantel in the parlor.

Cully looked at her, "thank ya Ma'am." Cully walks over to Walker on the floor. He leans down and looks at the leg, you're lucky Mz. Crawford's a bad shot, she didn't aim to shoot your leg off."

Liz looks at him. "Oh but I would have Mr. Cully. but then I thought that would mean blood all over my clean floor and with Mr. Crawford coming home today, well, it just was not happening."

Cully looked at her, then Liss as he helps Walker to a chair and grabs the rope that had tied Liss to the chair. "Now I know you are injured and all and it's only a small bullet in your leg, but I just want to make sure you don't get any notions on moving from this spot. Because if you do, I will shoot you in the leg and I have no problem with shooting the leg clean off, blood on the floor or not."

Liss looks at him, "well can't we at least tie up his leg?"

Liz looks at her, "he's fine."

SUDDENLY, THE SOUND of horse approaching means Waco and the men are back.

Liss heads out the door and waits on the porch as Waco stops to greet her. "Afternoon Mz. Liss, everything okay?"

She smiles at him, "well, it was alright until Mr. Walker came and wanting his wages, then tied us up and...."

Before she could finish, Waco was off his horse and running into the house. "Mz. Crawford! Mz. Crawford!"

"I'm right here Waco, not to worry, Mr.Walker is sitting here just waiting for someone to take him into town to see the doc."

Waco looks at the blood that has now dried on the pant leg. "Well, seems to me you had a slight accident here."

Walker looked at him, "I ain't saying nothing."

Waco looked at him, "Oh if I was you, I would really say something, anything 'cause the way it looks, you may be in for more trouble than you can handle."

Liss looks at Waco, "maybe we should wait till my pa gets home, he can explain why his study is destroyed."

Waco slowly walked to the study and looked in. Books, awards, figures all scattered across the floor, the drawers of his desk opened and the contents scattered around the floor. He just shook his head and walked back to the dining room. "The way I see it Walker, you got two choices, you can stay here and the judge deal with you or we can take you into town and let the sheriff deal with you. Mind you, either way is not gonna go well for you."

Walker looks at him, "I got nothing to say, but that woman shot me and I've got the bullet here in my leg."

"You meaning to say that Mz. Crawford, the judge's wife, took a gun and shot you for no reason at all."

"That's what I'm saying."

Liss looks at the window and sees her pa and the men approaching the house. She slowly makes her way out of the room into the hall and out the door to greet her father and Jason. With a smile on her face and a hearty wave, somehow, Eli knew something was not right. Oh, it was a fact that Liss always greeted them when they came back, but for some reason, she was a bit too showy, something was wrong.

Eli gets off his horse and his daughter rushes into his arms, "welcome home Papa."

Eli grabs her and gives her a big hug, then puts her down. "How's my fave girl an did you behave yourself?"

She looked at her pa. "I've been fine Papa, but there was a bit of trouble."

He looked at her, "and that being?"

She looked over at Jason who is smiling, just imagining what she will say next. Well Papa, I took Goldie out for a ride and she threw me." She closed her eyes and waited for Eli's reaction.

He looked at her still with her eyes closed, "You mean to tell me you rode that horse after we discussed the subject and agreed you would not ride her until I said so?"

She looked at him, "I know Papa, but if you had seen how lonely she looked in the stall."

"None the less young lady, did you not promise me you would not ride that horse!"

"Yes, I did Papa, but Papa..."

He looked at her, "Liss, I have been very fair with you, but you have got to hold up..." He looked up at his wife in the doorway. "Mrs. D"

Liz smiles at him, "Mr. Crawford, would you please come in here, there is a matter of great importance inside."

He follows her in, followed by Liss and Jason into the living room. where he stops in his tacks. "Walker!! What in Sam hill are you doing here and tied to one of my chairs?" He looks to his side and sees Cully smiling and giving him a nod. He looks again at Walker, "Mr. Walker, I asked you a question."

Walker looked at him, "Judge, you are married to a crazy woman. Just look at my leg, she shot me in the leg!"

Eli looked at his leg. "Yes, I see you have been shot and I'm sure there was a valid reason for her to shoot you, now just to get me on the same page with all of you, can you tell me why she shot you?"

Walker looks at him, "I was getting to that Judge. Well, you remember last time we spoke and you did say you would pay me when you got back to the ranch."

"I also remember you stating you couldn't wait that long and you then rode off.'"

Walker nods, "yes well, it came to me that if you would pay me at the ranch, it was a fact the money would be at the ranch now."

Eli started to smile and Walker began to smile, "so you thought you'd come to the house early and wait for me here."

Walker starting to laugh nervously. "So here you are coming early to wait for me to pay you."

"That's right, I come here and was just waiting for you."

Eli looks at him. "Why do I not find that believable since my study, as I am told is in shambles." Eli looks at Cully, "young man, I don't believe we've met."

Cully extends his hand out, "Michael Patrick Callahan JR, but everyone calls me Cully Sir.'"

Eli was very pleased at his presence and manners. "Pleased to meet you young man," he looks at Jason, "do you suppose you and Chet can take our friend Walker here, into town to enjoy the accommodations at our fine jail. Oh by the way, do stop at Doc Witherspoon, wouldn't want him to get a nasty infection with that wound."

"Sure thing Judge no problem."

With Waco's help, they remove him from the house and take him down to the stable where he can ride into town. He looks back at Cully,

"well Mr. Cully. Let's have an interesting talk on how you helped my little girl."

As if on cue, Liss appears behind them, "Papa?"

Eli turns and looks at her, "I believe you can help your mother."

"But Papa!!"

"Maybe next time you'll obey my rules. Look, if you promise to go help your mother, maybe we'll have some time before supper to exercise that horse of yours."

"Oh Papa, do you mean it"

"Only if you go help you mother, now off you go." She turns and walks back into the dining room and Eli opens the door to the study. He wasn't quite ready for what he was about to see. His law books. as well as others scattered all over the floor and torn. Plaques and honors thrown on the floor. even pictures on his desk were tossed on the floor or in the fireplace, the frames shattered. Slowly, Eli made his way to his chair, it was a fine leather chair at one time, now it was ripped to shreds. "Find yourself a place to set Son."

Cully sits down on what once was a fine chair.

Eli smiles. "well, suppose you tell me how you got hooked up with Liss. I know you've told the story a few times, but you have to understand, I just got here, so to speak and I also know my daughter and her ways."

Cully looks at the man, though he's told the story twice already he might as well start to tell it again, not that it would change. "Well Sir, I was riding down the trail when I noticed a fine young horse standing there on the trail behind a large tree limb, I looked toward the right and noticed what I thought was a young boy lying on the ground."

Eli looked at him, "a boy!"

"Yes Sir, well you see Sir, all I saw was a figure lying face down on the ground, I had no idea it was a girl. I mean she dresses like a teen age boy who would know."

The judge had to agree, "continue."

"Well Sir, I turned her over and realized not only she was a girl, but had a bad cut on her head. She was coming to, but still not steady to get up. She managed to tell me she lived around here and I offered to take her to her ranch. I helped her on the horse and saw she was still a bit shaky, so I tied her hands to the saddle horn so at least she wouldn't fall and I took the reins and led the horse in the direction she pointed to. It was slow going and I wasn't sure how long she could stay on the horse and then the rain started. Wasn't long before the trail looked like a stream and it was near impossible to go on. It was then I saw the dim light from a cabin not too far off on the left. I wasn't sure what to expect but I knew I had to get us to some shelter. I got to the cabin and an older man invited us in, said his name was Doctor Woodward, he took us in and tended to Mz. Liss' head wound and let her rest the night in his room. He and I spent the night in the outer room and in the morning, we headed toward your ranch."

Eli looked at the boy, then toward a box on his desk. Opening it, he takes out a cigar, then offers it to Cully.

"No Sir, I don't smoke."

"Well you won't mind if...'"

"Not at all."

He lit the cigar, then sat back and looked across the desk toward Cully. "Well your story was very interesting and I do thank you for helping my daughter." He smiles at the thought of him thinking she was a boy. "I, also, find it interesting that you met Doctor Woodward."

"Yes, it was a stroke of luck that I happened to see his cabin light in the rain."

Eli looked at him, extremely luck,"

Cully looked at him, "Sir?"

"Well you see it's the good doctor."

Cully looked at him, "I assure you Sir, he was there and ..."

Eli looked at the boy, "oh I'm sure he was, but..." He looked at him, "the doctor was there, he and his wife had moved to the territory before most of us. He started a small practice and was doing well. Oh, not like the doctor we have in town, well, it was about fifteen years ago, a year or two before me and the missus come out here. There was an epidemic, practically wiped out the town, Doc Woodward and his wife began treated folks at their home, then Mrs. Woodward came down with it. Well, he took care of her, best he could, but it just didn't do any good. She passed after about a week. The towns folk blamed the doctor for the epidemic, back then, an epidemic like that drove normal folk wild with anger and rage. they rode over to his cabin one night and shot him, then set fire to the cabin."

Cully looked at him, "you mean to ..."

"I'm only telling a story Son, one that you can believe or not, but it's the truth."

Cully still was not sure what to believe, after all, he spoke with the man. A man who was very much alive and now he is being told...

Eli looked at him, "Son, could you take me to the cabin tomorrow before you head off to the fort?"

He looks at the judge, "I will Sir."

Eli smiles at him. "fine. Well, shall we go and have some supper?"

Cully shakes his head and as Eli opens the door, he spots Liss sitting at a nearby chair. She walks up to her father, "well, it's about time you've come out. Supper is ready, but Mama wouldn't let me yell for you. Said you were busy. Told her you were just talking to Mr. Cully but she told me not to bother you."

Eli put his hand on her shoulder, "and she was right. Now let's get to the table."

Liss looks at Cully and smiles, "did you have a nice chat with my papa?"

"Very."

She smiles at him, "wanna tell me?"

"Not really." He smiles and continues walking into the next room.

Liz looks at Eli, "whatever do you think Mr. Cully told Liss?"

"Don't know, but I'm betting this boy won't be leaving in the morning."

As Liz walks into the room, Cully holds the chair for her to sit down. "Thank you Mr. Cully."

Liss stands by her chair, yet Cully makes no move toward her until Liss clears her throat. He looks at her and then walks over to her and holds the chair as she sits down.

Eli looks at Liz and smiles. Through the rest of the meal, the conversation was just routine, it was Liz'z question that opened a new conversation. She simply asked if Cully was planning to continue west after his trip to Fort Bennett.

"I really hadn't thought about it Ma'am. I have heard that further west is really nice and well, I've lived back east all my life and... well, I haven't given it much thought."

"Well what's wrong with Montana?," suddenly was heard from Liss's voice.

"Why nothing, nothing at all. It's a pleasant spot."

Liss gets up and heads out the door and to the barn.

Cully looks at Eli, "Sr?"

The old man nods. It's not you Son, it's well... Eli gets up and heads out to the barn.

Liz looks at Cully, "please don't worry, Liss can be a little headstrong at times."

Cully smiles, "Oh I understand Ma'am, but I hate to think I brought this on."

Liz looks at him, "don't be silly Mr. Cully, you did no such thing." She looks up as Eli comes back into the room.

"Well she's bottled herself up in the stall with her horse, most likely she'll spend the night there." Eli looks at Cully, "she's fine Son."

Chapter 8

It was sometime later when Cully made his way down the stairs and out to the barn, he couldn't just let her stay out there. He kept telling himself it wasn't his fault even the judge and Mz. Liz told him not to worry, but still, well somehow, he felt if he had answered her question differently, she would not have left. He had to at least try to make her understand.

Slowly. he made his way to the barn when he heard her voice, she was talking to the horse, from inside the stall, he saw her shadow sitting near the horse, "ya know Goldie, I really don't understand folks. Heck, I didn't say anything wrong, all I said was what's wrong with Montana! Now I tell ya what's so wrong with that? Why, we's as good a folk as them there in Fort Bennett. 'Sides, what do they have in that old fort that we ain't got here?

She was unaware that Cully was standing there until he spoke with a voice almost like a whisper, "Well for one thing, Fort Bennett doesn't have you."

Liss turns and sees him standing there. "You shouldn't be eavesdropping. T'aint polite."

He moves closer in the stall and smiles at her, "well now, that's a fine way to treat a body who comes down to make sure you are alright. I have a good mind to go back up and...'"

She stops him, "you came down to see if I was alright?"

He nods his head.

"Well that's mighty nice of you." She looks up at him, "Mr. Cully, did you really mean it when you said that Fort Bennett doesn't have me?"

He leans down and smiles at her, "I wouldn't say it if I didn't mean it. Besides I think Goldie kinda agrees with me."

"Oh now you're telling me what my horse would say," she stops for a minute, "did my papa send you out here?"

"Nope"

"You meaning to tell me you came out here all on your own?"

He smiles, "yep!"

She moves closer to him, "so you just come out here to see if'in I was alright."

He steps back a few steps as Liss was getting a bit too close. "Well yes, I knew it would be cold tonight and out here with…"

She moved closer to him, "well, there are blankets here in the barn and…" She puts her arms around his neck and then Cully gently removes them. "Well I think you should head up back to the house, if you want to come with us tomorrow."

Suddenly, the smile on her face was gone, and with a voice sounding like the word was impending doom, she repeated the word, "tomorrow."

Cully takes her hand and leads her out of the stall, closes its door and walks her up to the house. They walked hand in hand and in silence, with Liss keeping her eyes down.

Once inside the house she looks at him. Somehow, she will have to accept the fact he will be leaving sometime tomorrow and probably never see her again. *Why? Why did this have to happen? If she hadn't taken Goldie out she never would have had the accident and he would have never met her. But she did go out with Goldie and she did have the accident and he was on that road.*

They slowly climb the stairs together, Cully looks at her, yet she is strangely silent. When they reach the top of the steps and at the door to Liss' room, she looks up at him, "I'll miss you."

Cully looks down at her, he meant what he said, *Fort Bennett didn't have her and he'd give anything in the world to stay here with her but.* He gently lowers his head and brushed his lips to hers.

Her arms went around his neck and a simple kiss became much more.

It was Cully who had to gently take her arms from his neck and open the door to her room and gently push her in.

She looked at him not knowing what she did wrong, "what did?"

He smiled at her, "you get some rest. I'll talk to you in the morning." He gently closed the door and walked across the hall to his room, once inside, he shakes his head and smiles. One thing's for sure, Fort Bennett didn't have Liss. He doubted there was any other place that would have someone like Liss. He sat on the bed; the memory of her face came to his mind. Though he had only met her two days ago, she had crept into his mind, taken hold of his soul and though it sounds crazy, he, right now would rather stay here on this ranch than anywhere else on God's green earth. Call him touched in the head, but this slip of gal with her bewitching eyes found without knowing it had found a piece if his soul and was not letting go. He leaned back looking up at the ceiling until sleep finally took over.

He was awakened the next morning by the sound of light tapping on the door and Eli's voice, "Cully, breakfast is ready, you've got a busy day." He hears the judge leave and slowly opens the door and looks out into the hall. Slowly, he closes the door to the room and with his saddle bag and hat, heads down the stairs. He walks in to see Eli and Liss. "Good morning folks.'"

Eli smiles at him. "I trust you had a good night's rest."

He looks at him, "yes fine Judge." He looks at Liss and smiles and she smiles back at him. A reaction that was unnoticed by the judge, but then the judge liked the boy and he was kind enough to stop and help Liss. With breakfast done, the three head for the barn and saddle up.

As they slowly make their way out of the barn, Eli looks at Cully, "well you're the one who found it a few nights ago; I guess it's you who will lead the way now."

Cully nods and the three head down the path and toward the trail. Cully found the easiest way to find the cabin since he did not know the area was to start back at where he found Liss. Though the tree limb was now on the side of the road, it did create a slight problem of which direction he took to find help. "I'm not sure of the route Sir, but I know it was near the water."

Eli nodded, "that would be south Son. There's a stream not too far from here on the left side."

The left side registered to him, he remembered hearing the sound of water on his left. Slowly, Cully made his way slightly ahead of them being the last time he was on this trail there was not only dark, but he was facing he rain and slight flooding. He looked around, but there were no signs that looked familiar or anything that resembled a cabin. Half way through, Cully had a feeling his idea of direction was wrong and maybe they should be heading back. He was just about to turn when he turns the bend and sees the cabin. There, as big as big as life was the doctor's cabin, not more than fifty yards from him. He smiles at Liss and Eli, "there it is. Just like I remembered."

Liss smiles and they slowly make their way up to the cabin. Cully was the first to get off his horse and he made his way the door and gently knocks on the door. When no one answered, he tried again. It was then that the sound of a wagon approaching and Doc Woodward driving it caught Cully's attention. "Doc. Woodward!"

The old man smiles at them and walks over to them. "Well, well how are you folks? Miss Liss, how's your head feeling? Is this young man helping you ?" He looks at Eli and smiles, "Doctor Benjamin Woodward Sir, you must be Liss' dad."

Eli extends his hand to the gentleman, "Elias Crawford here and yes, I'm Liss' dad. I wanted to thank you personally for all you did for Liss."

The old man smiled, "well that's mighty kind of you coming all this way, but I was just doing my job. She mended nicely and look at her today, why you'd never know two days ago this was the gal her hubby brung here to get out of the rain."

Eli looked at Liss, then back to the doc, "well she has a mind of her own and she took off on that horse."

The doc looked at him, "well where's my manners, standing out here when I should be letting you all in." He opened the door and followed them in the house. Once inside, everything was the way it was two nights ago. "Have a seat Miss Liss, last time you were here you spent you time in the other room."

He looked at Eli. "Mr. Crawford, I tell you this son in law of yours never left the gal's sight. Why he even slept on the floor near the bed in case she woke up in the night." The old man gave a smile to Cully, then back to Eli.

Meanwhile, Eli looked at both Cully and Liss; it seemed this was something both of them had overlooked to tell him. Like why did the doctor get the impression that they were married and why did they not tell him they shared the same room. He smiles at the doctor, "there's something I've been wondering about. I heard of a Doc Woodward, but the story goes is that there was a fine doctor who came out here twenty years ago with his wife and set up a practice in town. This of course was before me and my wife came out. Anyway, there was an epidemic and the doctor as the story goes was tending the folks in town when his wife came down with the epidemic. The towns folk started blaming the doc for not getting rid of the fever. They set out for his place determined to stop it from spreading any further. Story has it that a group of some fine townsfolk, men mostly went out to the cabin well gave the doctor a chance to leave, but he didn't, so they shot him and set fire to the cabin. They watched it burn the ground then left." He looks at the old man, "now you still insist you are Doc Woodward?"

The old man looked at him without blinking, "I have no reason to lie, Mr. Crawford. I am Doctor Woodward and this is my cabin or should I say a replica of my cabin." he continued, "oh the townsfolk did come to the cabin, and there was a gentleman there, but it wasn't me. One of the settlers about thirty miles from here came to tell me his family had come down with the sickness, I offered him to rest at my place while I went to care for his folks. I had been gone only a day when the townsfolk came to the cabin. They shot him down and set fire to the place."

Eli looked at him.

"They shot an innocent man and burned down my home, I figured the best thing to do was to stay dead."

Eli spoke up, "but there are people who say they had seen you and well, when Liss told us all about the good doctor, I got to thinking maybe this ghost everyone talks about isn't really a ghost at all. Tell me Doctor, how have you been surviving all these years?"

The man looks at him, "well those folks I went to help that evening have been more than kind, they found this piece of land and with their own money purchased it for me and built this cabin just like the one I lost. And yes, I did care for others who needed help like you two. Tell you the truth, I really didn't think I'd see you again."

Liss smiles and chuckles, "well you see you don't know my papa."

With that remark, they all start to laugh.

Cully looked at the doctor, "since we're cleaning up stories here, I guess it's my turn. You see Doc, me and Liss aren't newlyweds, heck, we never saw each other until I found her on the road. I was trying to get her home when the rain started and well... You were so kind to us and we thought we'd never see you again and..."

Liss looked at him, "we wanted you not to think we were doing anything..."

The doctor looked at them both and smiled, "let me tell both you that night I saw two people who needed help, and together they formed a bond that not even the good Lord would find fault with. You kids came back knowing you would have to tell me the truth and that took courage. I admired that in you. Mr. Crawford, you have been blessed with a special daughter who will be a remarkable lady one day." He looks at Cully and whispers in his ear, "don't let her slip away Son."

It was later that afternoon when Eli and the others were getting ready to head back home; they stood outside the doc's cabin and promised to stop by again.

Reluctant they mounted their horses knowing at the end of the trail they would once again part ways.

Cully still had to deliver a message to Fort Bennett.

They got to the fork and Eli looks at Cully, "well Son, it looks like this is where we part company for only a spell I hope." He extends his hand and smiles, "I'll give you two some time to say goodbye, I'll be over there near the stream to give you some privacy." He smiles at Cully and slowly rides off.

Cully looks at Liss, suddenly he can't find the words to say how he feels. *Why, how would it sound only knowing a gal for three days and saying he loves her. Why it ain't so like no one would believe it. 'Sides Liss is a girl from fine folks.*

Liss looks at him, "well, are you gonna say goodbye or just sit there?"

He smiles at her. Just when he tries to find those tender words all women like to hear, she comes out with that tomboy scarcasm. "Maybe I don't or won't say goodbye."

She looks at him and he notices the hint of tears starting to form. Tears, why he never wanted to make her cry. Why she was just a gal who.... A single tear rolled down her cheek and Cully looked at her. "Now why did you have to go and do that? I didn't mean to make you cry. Look if you want me to say good bye to you, I will, just don't cry. Come on Liss, stop crying." He couldn't stop the tears, "Liss I promise when I am done at Fort Bennett, I'll come back and see you."

She looked at him, "you're just saying that."

He took her hand in his, "no I'm not, I promise I'll come back here."

A slight smile comes to her face, "you promise? Cross your heart?"

He smiled at her, "cross my heart and hope to..."

She put her hand to his mouth, "oh no don't say it. Please don't say hope to die. I couldn't bear it if anything happened to you, not now.'"

He leaned over and gently kissed her cheek, "Melissa Crawford, you have my promise, I will be back." With that he slowly makes his way down the trail and Liss joins her father.

Chapter 9

It was two days before Cully made it to Fort Bennett. He got to the fort late that afternoon. As the gates opened and Cully rode in, he was greeted by the second in command. He looks at Cully, "your business here?"

"I have a dispatch for Captain Stiles from Washington."

The officer looks at him, we've been expecting you Major Cullhan. The captain is in his office."

Cully smiles and heads toward the captain's office. He dismounts and heads for the door.

Inside the inner office, Captain Stiles was sitting at his desk when his orderly knocked on the door and upon opening the door announces Mr. Cullhan is here. The captain gets up. "Cully, good to see you."

"Been a long time Doug."

They sit down and the captain continues, "I was expecting you two days ago."

Cully smiles, "well I got a bit sidetracked about wo days ride from here."

The captain looks at him, "was she blonde, brunette, or red head."

Cully smiles, "well let's just say I promised her I'd see her again."

Both men smile.

Cully reaches in his pocket and takes out an envelope and hands it to the captain. "I believe this is what you are waiting for."

The captain opens the envelope and begins reading the paper. He looks up at Cully, "do you know what is in this?"

He nods his head yes.

"Then you know what is expected by all of us."

"Yes sir, I have orders to find and escort all prospectors out of the hills and keep them out until there can be sort of peace."

The captain looked at him, "you know that will take longer than a few weeks?"

"I am fully aware of that, but these are the orders I was given."

The captain looked at him, "then tell me one thing, my friend, at what price do we have to pay to carry out these orders? How many deaths on both sides will convince those back in Washington that this is not a civilized territory?"

The memory of the Big Horn still is fresh in our minds, many of those men had families who had moved out here to be where their loved ones died. What's the real reason Cully? Or is it you've joined in with them and their side or lies and coverups."

Cully left the captain's office later that evening. He walked about the fort thinking of his friend's words. Had he indeed turned into the group of men he had hated years ago? Were all the rights and beliefs he once had been tossed aside for a new set of values. He also thought about Liss, he promised her he'd be back; did the wishes of Washington mean more than his promise to her? He looked up at that full moon shining down. That same moon was shining down on her and it was then he knew what he had to do. Blame it all on that full moon or the Montana Magic, but he was going back and find a better way.

THE END

Also by Louise Riveiro-Mitchell

Autumn Series
Cheyenne Autumn Sky
The Dark Skies Over Autumn
Autumn's Promise

Custer's Gold
Custer's Gold
Gold Is Where You Find It

Magic Series
Montana Magic

Standalone
The Path of Buck Cross
In A Land Where Dreams Come True
Summer Wind

About the Author

Louise Riveiro -Mitchell started writing in her teens. Growing up in the 60's she became fond of westerns and one could find her sitting on a chair watching whatever western was on. The Virginian, The Tall, Laramie, Wagon Train, Laredo etc. She started to pick up their vernacular and at times people find it hard to believe she's from New York. She write her first book in 2001 and if it wasn't for her late husband's insistence it would never have lead to others and two poetry books. She has also ghostwritten over 37 historical westerns. Not only does she love the genre she finds that era in our history interesting. She lives in Westchester County New York and have two children and three grandchildren. And still watches those westerns from years ago.

About the Publisher

Outlaws Publishing is a family-oriented organization.

What I mean by that is, we as a family will help one another in all aspects of our work. Now we all know that families squabble, fuss and might even come to fisticuffs at times, but if someone jumps on one of the members of our family, then they have to take on all of us. We may not like one another at times, but when we get to the bottom line, we do care about and love one another.

That's all fine, you may say, but it doesn't really tell me what Outlaws Publishing is going to do for me to make my book a success.

If you are a Western Writer that often feels as if no one cares. If you feel overlooked and discounted? If you feel like you aren't getting the credit that you deserve?

Well, don't think you are the only one who has those feelings. Western novelist quite often do not get the credit they deserve.

But in today's new world of publishing, Western Books have the potential to become one of the leading sellers in today's book market. Your story could very well be the one at the top of the best sellers list with the help of Outlaws Publishing.

Outlaws Publishing has the experience, the expertise, the contacts and the power to put your Western Novel at the top of the best sellers list Outlaws Publishing believes Western Authors have HUGE potential. Outlaws Publishing is looking for Western writers to join our rapidly growing family of successful authors.

Make the move today to Outlaws Publishing.

Join the growing ranks of Western writers looking for success by hanging your spurs in the bunkhouse at Outlaws Publishing.